DISCARD

A Break-of-Day Book

Ever since 1928, when Wanda Gág's classic *Millions of Cats* appeared, Coward-McCann has been publishing books of high quality for young readers. Among them are the easy-to-read stories known as Break-of-Day books. This series appears under the colophon shown above — a rooster crowing in the sunrise — which is adapted from one of Wanda Gág's illustrations for *Tales from Grimm*.

Though the language used in Break-of-Day books is deliberately kept as clear and as simple as possible, the stories are not written in a controlled vocabulary. And while chosen to be within the grasp of readers in the primary grades, their content is far-ranging and varied enough to captivate children who have just begun crossing the momentous threshold into the world of books.

Coward-McCann, Inc.

New York

Who's Afraid
of
Ernestine?

by Marjorie Weinman Sharmat
pictures by Maxie Chambliss

Library of Congress Cataloging in Publication Data
Sharmat, Marjorie Weinman.
Who's afraid of Ernestine?
Summary: Cecil is afraid of his awesome classmate
Ernestine, who makes firm attempts to get him
over to her house for "surprises."
[1. Fear—Fiction] I. Chambliss, Maxie, ill. II. Title.
PZ7.S5299Wj 1986 [E] 85-14911
ISBN 0-698-30746-1
First impression.

To Lil and Hy
and a friendship that's pure Silver
MWS

For Gabe + Emma ♥ Max

I, Cecil Albert Fingle,
am afraid of Ernestine Rindblatt.

When I see her coming,
I try to hide.
But every day
she sees me across the playground.
She runs over, gives me a poke,
and tries to grab my hand.

That's bad enough.
But last week
disaster finally happened.
What I have dreaded the most.
A school project.
Ernestine and I are teamed up
to write a composition together.

The amazon and the coward.
And, even worse, Ernestine
wants to do it at her house.
And that scares me
as much as Ernestine scares me
because yesterday I went to her house.
I thought I was brave.
I found out I was stupid.

When I got there,
Ernestine opened the door so fast,
it hit me in the nose.
While I was rubbing my nose,
Ernestine grabbed my hand.
That hurt worse than my nose.

"I have lots of surprises for you,"
she said.
"But first come in and
meet my new dog, Killer."
I turned and ran.
I'm not that stupid.
Ernestine yelled after me,
"Hey, come back soon!"

I hope Ernestine has heard of never.

She hasn't.
Ernestine is after me again today.
Here she comes.
She's going to sit right beside me
in the cafeteria.

That's what *she* thinks.
I, Cecil Albert Fingle,
know how to crawl.
I am taking my lunch
and crawling two tables away.

Ernestine is looking for me
at eye level.
I am not there.
I am clutching the floor.
I am pretending
I lost part of my lunch.

At last she gives up and sits down.
Her back is to me.
I stand up. I am safe.
I eat lunch two tables away
from Ernestine.
I eat quickly.
I leave the cafeteria
before she does.

Now Ernestine will try
to sit beside me in English.
She will not succeed.
I stand at a distance
while everyone goes into class.
Including Ernestine.
After she sits down,
I go into class.
I take the empty seat
farthest away from Ernestine.
At least ten heads and ten bodies
separate me from her.
But I slouch low in my seat
just in case.
When class is over, I rush out.

It is time to go home.
Ernestine always tries to catch up
with me on the way home.
There are many hiding places
between school and my house.

Ernestine has found me
in all of them.

I start to run.
I hear someone running behind me.
I do not look back.
I run faster.
I am running for a good cause.

My safety.

I tell myself
that I can outrun Ernestine.
I tell myself
that my feet have wings
and Ernestine's have bricks.
I hear brick feet catching up to me.
"C-E-C-I-L! Come back to my house.
I have lots of surprises for you."
Ernestine is calling me.
It sounds like a roll of thunder
and a crash of lightning.
It sounds like doom.

"E-R-N-E-S-T-I-N-E!"
Someone is calling Ernestine.
I hear brick feet stop.
Ernestine is waiting for someone.
I, Cecil Albert Fingle,
am not waiting.

I run home.

I am safe. For today.
But tomorrow I have to go back
to Ernestine's house
and write the composition.
Tomorrow I have to spend
the whole morning with Ernestine,
several pencils and papers,
and great fear.
Maybe tomorrow won't come.

I stay up as late as I can.
When I finally go to bed
and fall asleep,
I dream about Ernestine.

She is a dragon lady
with green talons,
hanging teeth,
and a flowing cape.
She looks better than
she has ever looked.

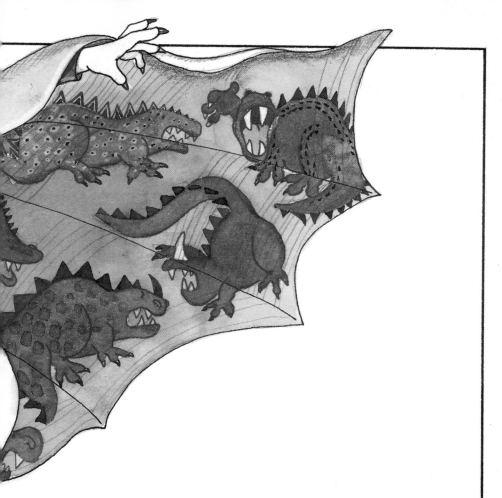

Her lips are scarlet.
Her hair is black.
It looks as if it has been chopped
with a hatchet.
She is definitely looking better.
But she has an unfortunate hobby.

She sucks blood like a vampire.
Then she bottles it
and sells it as tomato juice.
She gives away free saltines
with every bottle.

I have found out all these things
about Ernestine
and I have been asleep
for only one minute.

I wake up. Morning.
I would like to skip morning
and move directly to afternoon.

But I can't.

I leave my house.
I walk slowly.

I am three blocks
from Ernestine's house
when I think I see her
waiting for me.

She is dressed in red tights
that reveal more muscles
than I knew she had.
Her pitchfork, of course, is black.
She does not look good in horns,
but I will not tell her that.

Ernestine flicks her tail.
She is eager to see me.
I am made of marshmallows
and pink feathers.

Then she's gone.

Two blocks.

One block.

I am walking up
to Ernestine's front door.

I ring the bell.
No answer. I know why.
Ernestine is busy inside
with her surprises.

She is bent over her cauldron.
She is wearing a dark robe with a hood.
A wart is growing on her nose
while she sprinkles herbs and
squeezes strange ointments from tubes.
She peers into the cauldron
and stirs everything around
with a long stick.
Now her brew is finished.
I will be forced to drink it,
and it will make me break out
in green spots
and give me hiccups forever.

Ernestine opens the door. Slowly.

She has changed her clothes.
She is not wearing
a dark robe with a hood.
She is wearing blue jeans.
She is smiling. No hanging teeth.

"Hi, Cecil," she says.
"Come on in."
She gives me a little poke,
a little hand grab.
But gentle.

I walk inside.

I look for her dog, Killer.
I find him.
Killer is a toy poodle.
He is wagging his toy tail.

Ernestine has poured lemonade.
Two glasses.

Ernestine has laid out
pencils, erasers, and papers.
She lets me sit in the big chair.
Ernestine is so nice to me.
She gives me a napkin
and a paper plate.
"I got us some munchies," she says.
I like munchies.

We write a composition
about wheat and oats.
I am wheat and Ernestine is oats.

She has many good ideas.
She even lets me use
her wheat thoughts.

We finish. Ernestine says,
"I'll see you tomorrow."
That doesn't sound too bad.

I walk home and
I think of Ernestine.
Ernestine likes me. I know it.
Ernestine makes me lemonade
and gives me munchies.
Ernestine saves her pokes
and her grabs
and her wheat thoughts
for me.

She is making a terrible mistake.
I am not worth wheat thoughts
and lemonade and munchies.
I am horrible.
Horrible for thinking
all those horrible thoughts
about Ernestine.
I am a big, yellow blob
of spilled buttermilk.
I am a quivering, clutching jellyfish.
I am a cringing, nail-crunching coward.
I, Cecil Albert Fingle,
am everything I don't like.

One last thing about Ernestine.

She really likes
spilled buttermilk,
quivering jellyfish,
and nail-crunching cowards.

50308

JE
Sharmat, Marjorie Weinman.
Who's afraid of Ernestine?
$8.99